The Magic Cornfield

NANCY WILLARD

Tottem

Bottom

HARCOURT BRACE & COMPANY

San Diego   New York   London

Requests for permission to make copies of any part of the work should be mailed to: Permissions Department, Harcourt Brace & Company, 6277 Sea Harbor Drive, Orlando, Florida 32887-6777.

Stamp designs copyright © U.S. Postal Service. Reproduced with permission.

Braid doll (Hungry Horse, MT): Used with permission from Charla Khanna.

Doll with hat (Hat Creek, CA): Used with permission from Tracy Gallup.

Cheerleader dolls (What Cheer, IA): Used with permission from the Collegiate Doll Company, El Segundo, California.

Sculptures and other oddities created by the author.

Library of Congress Cataloging-in-Publication Data
Willard, Nancy.
The magic cornfield/Nancy Willard.
p. cm.
Summary: On his way to visit Cousin Bottom in Minneapolis, Cousin Tottem gets lost in a magic cornfield, from which he sends Bottom a series of postcards telling about his outlandish experiences.
ISBN 0-15-201428-4
[1. Letters—Fiction. 2. Magic—Fiction.] I. Title.
PZ7.W6553Mag 1997
[Fic]—dc20   96-24850

F E D C B A

Printed in Singapore

No ducks, chickens, angels, horses, or other creatures were harmed in the making of these pictures.

The cover type was hand lettered and electronically adapted by John Stevens.
The text was hand lettered by Eileen Boniecka.
Title page portraits photographed by On Location, Poughkeepsie, New York
Color separations by United Graphic Pte Ltd., Singapore
Printed and bound by Tien Wah Press, Singapore
This book was printed on totally chlorine-free Nymolla Matte Art paper.
Production supervision by Stanley Redfern and Ginger Boyer
Designed by Judythe Sieck

THE MAGIC CORNFIELD

For James, who made it to Minneapolis

Dear Tottem,   Minneapolis, MN
                                June 1

Here's hoping you can join me in
Minneapolis on September 1 for my
100th birthday. I'm sending along
that snapshot I took of us last
year, when you turned 99. Why not
come a few weeks early so we can enjoy
the garden before the weather turns cold?
I'll order our favorite angel meringue pie.

                    Your loving cousin,
                    Bottom Perhaps

somewhere in New York

Dear Bottom,

I'm on my way, but two hours after I left home my car broke down. There was nothing but a cornfield to the east and west of me, and not another car in sight. So I headed into the corn, looking for someone to help me, and found, of all things, a mailbox with this sign on it:

DROP YOUR MESSAGE INTO THIS
    TRAVELING MAILBOX.
  IT WILL BE TRANSFERRED
  TO A POSTCARD AND DELIVERED
    TO ITS DESTINATION.
  THE TRAVELER'S AID BUREAU
      OF THE MAGIC CORNFIELD

I'll leave my message in the box to see if it works. I've been walking for hours. Wish I could curl up and take a nap.

Your footsore cousin,
Tottem Perhaps

Bottom Perhaps
P.O. Box 3811
Minneapolis,
    MN
    55403

Sleepy Eye, MN

Dear Bottom,
   I just woke up
from the longest
nap of my life.
The cornfield
is full of
sleepers. I
can't see them,
but every leaf and tassel is
shaking with snores.
   Oh, to be in a place where I
could hear the birds instead of
this racket. The mailbox seems
to have followed me here.
            Your wakeful cousin,
               Tottem

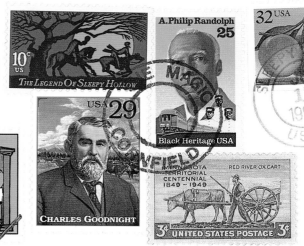

Bottom   Perhaps

P.O. Box 3B11

Minneapolis,

      MN

   55403

Bird-in-Hand, PA

Dear Bottom,
   The moment I
dropped my message in
the mailbox, the snoring
stopped, and I heard
the dither of peeping and
honking. A small duck flew
down and settled himself
beside me.
   "No one should try to
cross the Magic Cornfield
alone," said the duck. "Take
me with you to Minneapolis."
   The duck and I have been
walking all day. I'm ready to
turn in. I hope the sun shows
his face tomorrow morning.
       Your hopeful cousin,
       Tottem

Bottom Perhaps

P.O. Box 3Bll

Minneapolis,
       MN
       55403

Dear Bottom,
   It's a fine morning
but I feel terrible.
We've come to an
enormous lake, and
I don't know how
to swim.
   "Everyone should learn
to swim," said the duck,
"but the Magic Cornfield is
full of miracles. Pray for a miracle."
   The mailbox is here as usual,
so perhaps you'll get this message.
I'd love to know what these
postcards look like.
               Timidly yours,
               Tottem

Morning Sun, IA
"WE KEEP IT SHINING"
MORNING SUN
First Rural Route in the State
Established Nov. 10th 1896

MORNING SUN IA 52640
32 USA
AUG 24 1995
PM
USPS

THE MAGIC CORNFIELD

32 USA

USA 45
Pumpkinseed Sunfish

KANSAS STATEHOOD · 1861·1961 · U.S. POSTAGE

Bottom Perhaps

P. O. Box 3B11

Minneapolis, MN

               55403

Angels Camp, CA

Dear Bottom,
    Would you believe my luck? Three angels stopped by in a canoe to pick me up and carry me to the campground where angels take their vacations. The duck paddled behind us.
    After dinner, when it was time to leave, an angel warned us to watch out for the Hungry Horses.
    "They love whistling," said the angel. "Can you whistle 'Yankee Doodle'? It's their favorite."
    This sounds like nonsense to me. After walking all day, I long to hear a sensible voice, besides mine and the duck's.
                Nervously yours,
                Tottem

Bottom Perhaps
P.O. Box 3B11
Minneapolis,
        MN
    55403

Stamps, AR

Dear Bottom,
    No sooner had I dropped my last message into the mailbox than a hubbub of voices poured out of it. Peering through the slot, I saw all the stamps talking to each other.
    "Shocking news!" one stamp shouted. "A Hungry Horse broke a tooth trying to eat the mailbox!"
    If there's anybody in charge of this place, I'd like to meet that person. I hope I'm out of this field in time for your birthday. But I haven't a clue what day it is or where I am.
                    Your baffled cousin,
                        Tottem

Bottom Perhaps
P.O. Box 3B11
Minneapolis, MN
      55403

Dime Box, TX

Dear Bottom,
    I'm all alone again. The duck and I were traveling through the field minding our own business when a man jumped out of the cornstalks shouting, "A dime or your duck. I am the toll keeper."
    I didn't have a dime, so he grabbed the duck.
    "Don't worry," whispered the duck. "I'll fly away when he's got his back turned."
    I am very unhappy. I was growing fond of that duck. Without a guide, I feel lost.
    Oh, Bottom, have I missed your birthday?
            Morosely yours,
            Tottem

DIME BOX
SEP 5 P.M 1995
77853

THE MAGIC CORNFIELD

Bottom Perhaps
P.O. Box 3B11
Minneapolis,
    MN
    55403

Sistersville, WV

Dear Bottom,
    After walking in
circles for hours, I met
five little girls playing Hide-
and-Seek. When I told them
I was lost, they whispered
among themselves. At last
the oldest said," Have you
no sisters? When one of us
gets lost, the rest of us
hitch a ride with the clouds
so we can look down on the
field and find her."
    The clouds look comfortable
enough, but give me the earth
any day.
        Your earthbound cousin,
        Tottem

Bottom Perhaps
P.O. Box 3B11
Minneapolis,
        MN
    55403

Earth, Tx

Dear Bottom,
    A cloudburst has
turned the cornfield into
a mudfield. The earth
is drenched, and everything
wants to grow. You can't
even pick up a twig without
having it take root in
your hand.
    There's an awful
snorting and trampling
to the west. I hope the
Hungry Horses have
already eaten.
        Fearfully yours,
        Tottem

Bottom Perhaps
P.O. Box 3B11
Minneapolis,
      MN
    55403

Hungry
Horse, MT

Saddlebred

Quarter horse

Morgan

USA 13c Crazy Horse

Dear Bottom,
   When I saw two
horses galloping toward
me, I thought my last
hour had come. But they rushed
right past me. They were following
a little girl who was whistling
"Yankee Doodle."
   It's hot, hot, hot in the
cornfield. Not a shade tree in
sight. I wish I had a hat to
keep the sun off.
            Your sunbaked cousin,
               Tottem

Bottom Perhaps

P.O. Box 3811

Minneapolis,
MN
55403

Hat Creek, CA

SEP 8 1995 P.M
HAT CREEK CA

MAGIC CORNFIELD

Dear Bottom,
   Would you believe my bad luck?
I've been arrested for not
wearing a hat. Everybody in this
part of the cornfield is required
to wear one. When I told the
policeman that I left my hat
in the car a long time ago, he
didn't believe my story. Oh,
what will become of me? And
which way is Minneapolis?
         Your hatless cousin,
         Tottem

Bottom Perhaps
P.O. Box 3B11

Minneapolis,
         MN
         55403

Truth or Consequences, NM

Dear Bottom,
    So here I am in jail, waiting to defend myself. The poster in my cell says:
  THOU SHALT NOT STEAL. I have a toilet and a sink and a shelf for a bed. Nothing more. The mailbox is waiting for me outside the window. I'll throw my message through the bars.
    I wish I were wise enough to get myself out of this mess.
          Your captive cousin,
           Tottem

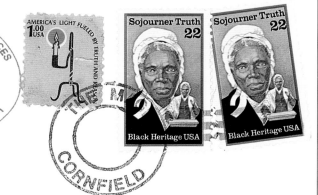

TRUTH OR CONSEQUENCES
SEP 8 1995
NM · USPS · 87901

CORNFIELD

AMERICA'S LIGHT FUELED BY TRUTH AND REASON
1.00 USA

Sojourner Truth 22
Black Heritage USA

Sojourner Truth 22
Black Heritage USA

Bottom Perhaps

P.O. Box 3B11

Minneapolis,
MN
55403

Wise River, MT

Dear Bottom,
      Last night as I was
dropping off to sleep, I heard
a voice whisper, "I am the
river that runs under the
jail. Pull out the big stone
in the floor under your bed
and follow me."
      Sure enough, there was the
stone. When I lifted it out,
I found a cavern with an
underground river, shallow
enough for me to wade in.
      So I'm walking the wise
river that came to help me.
            Your rescued cousin,
            Tottem

Bottom Perhaps
P. O. Box 3B11
Minneapolis, MN
            55403

Peculiar, MO

Dear Bottom,
        You'll never believe what I
saw today: a six-legged horse
with feathers, running over the snow.
        "Hello, old friend," called the
horse. "Don't you know who I am?"
        "No," I said. "I 've never seen
one like you before."
        "I am the duck. After I
escaped from the toll keeper, I fell
asleep, and when I woke up I
wasn't the same duck at all. Can
I still be your duck?"
        "You will always be my duck,"
I said, "no matter what you look
like on the outside."
        I'm weary with walking, and the
cornfield seems endless. We both need
cheering up.   Your cautious cousin,
                            Tottem

THE AGE OF REPTILES

PECULIAR MO
SEP
18
PM
1995
64078

USA 25 Pteranodon

USA 25 Stegosaurus

Bottom Perhaps

P.O. Box 3B11

Minneapolis,
            MN
        55403

What Cheer, IA

Dear Bottom,

    I feel like we're a parade.
Two young ladies are following us
and cheering us on.
    "How beautiful the snow is,"
said the feathered horse.
    "On the other hand," I said,
"a peep of green would be nice, to
show us the path."

       Cheerfully yours,
        Tottem

Bottom Perhaps

P.O. Box 3B11

Minneapolis,
      MN
     55403

Left Hand, WV

Dear Bottom,
   You have to be careful of words in this place. Right in the middle of the snow, I found a leaf with somebody's hand resting on it.
   "You said 'On the other hand'," said the duck. "It's the other hand."
   "Maybe it's a sign warning us of danger," I said. "Something hidden, like quicksand."

         Your puzzled cousin,
         Tottem

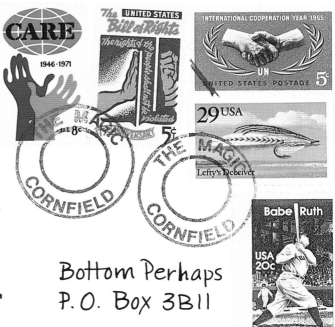

Bottom Perhaps
P.O. Box 3B11

Minneapolis,
   MN
  55403

Brothers, OR

Dear Bottom,
   Well, I've found the quicksand. Two angels who fell into it asked me to pull them out.
   "We have no quicksand where we live," they said, "so we are not used to it."
   I pulled one out, but the other stuck fast.
   "Keep trying," said the angel I'd saved. "I'm not free until my brother is."
   We tugged and pulled, and when the second angel sprang free, they thanked me, shook the mud from their wings, and flew away. The feathered horse was looking very downcast.
   "I wish I could meet another bird as peculiar as I am," he sighed.
                  Your fast-stepping cousin,
                     Tottem

Bottom Perhaps
P.O. Box 3B11
Minneapolis,
          MN
          55403

Chicken, AK

Dear Bottom,
    The feathered horse
has found himself a
family right in the middle
of the cornfield. He says
they're chickens.
    "Are you sure they're real birds?"
I asked. "They don't look like any
chickens I've ever seen."
    "And I don't look like any
duck you've ever seen," he
reminded me. "This is the Magic
Cornfield. Good luck on your
travels. I'll miss you."
    "And I'll miss you," I said. "Who else
has stuck with me the way you have?"
    "The moon," said the feathered
horse. "She makes all roads bright."
                Hopefully yours,
                Tottem

CHICKEN ALASKA
SEP
20
PM
1995
99732

HAPPY NEW YEAR!
29 USA

HAPPY NEW YEAR!
29 USA

Delaware
USA 20c
Blue Hen Chicken &
Peach Blossom

CHICKEN, AK
SEP
20
1995
USPS

1848 1948
CENTENNIAL OF THE
AMERICAN
POULTRY INDUSTRY
UNITED STATES POSTAGE 3¢

Bottom Perhaps
P.O. Box 3B11
Minneapolis, MN
    55403

Luna, NM

Dear Bottom,
    The moon is good company. She watches over me all night. I'm getting a bit tired of eating corn. It's a good thing the moon isn't made of green cheese.

          Your hungry cousin,
          Tottem

In the beginning God...

SIX CENTS · UNITED STATES

USA 29

First Moon Landing, 1969

LUNA, NM
SEP
22
AM
1995
87824

THE MAIL
CORNFIELD

Hispanic Americans

A Proud Heritage USA 20

Bottom Perhaps

P.O. Box 3B11

Minneapolis, MN
          55403

Shopville, KY

Dear Bottom,

The Magic Cornfield has everything, even a supermarket. But I have no money. I was looking for the manager to ask if he could help me when I bumped into an angel.

"I never expected to meet the likes of you in here," I exclaimed.

The angel laughed.

"We leave food baskets on the doorsteps of hungry families. Are you the traveler who saved my brother? Are you still looking for Minneapolis?"

I said yes.

"The angel who carries our baskets is swift. He will carry you to the border of the Magic Cornfield."

I'm keeping my fingers crossed.
                    Your joyful cousin,
                         Tottem

Bottom Perhaps
P.O. Box 3811
Minneapolis,
        MN
    55403

Happy, TX

Dear Bottom,
    The children
who play at the
border of the Magic
Cornfield laughed
when I told them
how long I've been
traveling.
    "You could have left the cornfield a
long time ago if you hadn't believed in magic,"
said one little girl. "Your car's outside the gate.
Take the first road north. You'll be in
Minneapolis by suppertime."
    Oh, Bottom, how delightful it will be,
sitting in your garden again! I hope you
saved me a piece of angel meringue pie.
                Your loving cousin,
                    Tottem

Bottom Perhaps
P.O. Box 3B11
Minneapolis,
        MN
        55403